Reading Gems

The Weather Monster

High up on a mountain lives the weather monster. When he is happy, the sun always shines.

When the weather monster is sad, it rains and it pours.

It has been raining a lot lately.

Quarto is the authority on a wide range of topics.

Quarto educates, entertains and enriches the lives of our readers—enthusiasts and lovers of hands-on living.

www.quartoknows.com

First published in 2018 by QED Publishing,
an imprint of The Quarto Group.
The Old Brewery, 6 Blundell Street,
London N7 9BH, United Kingdom.
T (0)20 7700 6700 F (0)20 7700 8066
www.QuartoKnows.com

A catalogue record for this book is available from the British Library.

ISBN 978-1-78493-929-8

Based on the original story by Steve Smallman and Bruno Merz
Author of adapted text: Katie Woolley
Series Editor: Joyce Bentley
Series Designer: Sarah Peden

Manufactured in Dongguan, China TL052018

9 8 7 6 5 4 3 2

MIX
Paper from responsible sources
FSC® C104723

FSC
www.fsc.org

The villagers are fed up with all the rain. They need a plan to cheer up the weather monster.

"We can bake him a cake!" says Joe, the baker's boy.

"Great idea," says his dad.

Everyone is too afraid to give the cake to the monster. Only Joe is brave enough.

Joe sets off up the mountain with the cake in his backpack. He walks and walks for miles.

At last, Joe arrives at the weather monster's cave.

The weather monster has been watching Joe climb the mountain. He opens his front door.

"Hello," he says. "I'm the weather monster but you can call me Ron."

"I'm Joe," says Joe. "Pleased to meet you."

"It's great to meet you, Joe," says Ron.
"What brings you this far up my mountain?"

"I've brought you some cake from the village," says Joe.

"Marvellous!" says Ron. "I'm feeling a bit peckish."

The weather monster and Joe sit down for a nice cup of tea and some cake.

Ron is so happy that he can't help grinning. Suddenly, it stops raining and the sun comes out.

Joe and the weather monster are soon chatting like old friends.

"This is fun," says Ron. "Why haven't any of the villagers come to visit me before?"

"Well, it's usually very sunny in the village so we don't need to bother you," says Joe. "Lately, it's been raining a lot and everyone is fed up. We thought a cake would cheer you up and bring back the sun!"

This makes the weather monster
very cross indeed.

"Sunshine!" he bellows. "All you want to
do is have some sun instead of rain."

Joe jumps up in fright, spilling his tea
everywhere.

The weather monster is getting
crosser and crosser. Thunder roars and
lightning flashes. Joe is scared.

Ron takes one look at Joe's scared face and stops shouting at once.

"I'm sorry," he sniffs. "I don't mean to scare you. I'm just very lonely up here all by myself. I hoped that maybe the villagers wanted to be my friends."

"I'm sure they do!" says Joe. "Come and meet everyone."

Joe and Ron set off back down the mountain. It doesn't take long with Ron carrying Joe all the way.

When the villagers see the weather monster, they are scared.

"Meet my friend, Ron," shouts Joe.

Ron grins his toothy grin and the sun comes out.

"Hello, everyone," he says.

One by one, the villagers begin to feel brave enough to meet Ron the weather monster.

Everyone sees that he isn't scary at all. Ron is just a bit different... in a good way!

"Come and live in the village with us," says Joe.

"Thank you," says Ron. "But I'm a bit too big to live here. Besides, I like my cave high up on the mountain."

At the end of the day, it's time for the weather monster to go back home.

Now the villagers take it in turns to visit him. They always bring him a cake or two!

He isn't the weather monster anymore. He is just their friend Ron.

Ron has never been happier and the sun is always shining!

Story Words

backpack

baker

cake

cave

front door

Joe

lighting

lonely

mountain

rain

Ron the weather monster

scared

sun

thunder

village

Let's Talk About The Weather Monster

Look carefully at the book cover.

What is the weather like?

What object in the picture gives a clue to the weather?

In the story, Ron the weather monster is lonely and left out.

Have you ever felt lonely or left out? What does it feel like?

Joe is scared of the thunder and lightning.

What things frighten you sometimes?

What can you do to stop feeling scared?

The story is all about rain and sunshine.

What other kinds of weather can you think of?

What is your favourite season?

What have Joe and Ron learnt by the end of the story?

Did you like the ending?

What do you think happened next?

Fun and Games

Look at the pictures and the words. Count the syllables in each word. Choose the correct number of syllables from the list below.

lightning

cake

weather monster

villagers

 4 2 3 1

Answers: lightning = 2 syllables; cake = 1 syllable; weather monster = 4 syllables; villagers = 3 syllables

Read these sentences.
Match them to the weather pictures below.

1. It has been raining a lot lately.

2. Thunder roars and lightning flashes.

3. Ron grins his toothy grin and the sun comes out.

4. Now the villagers take it in turns to visit him.

Your Turn

Now that you have read the story,
have a go at telling it in your own words.
Use the pictures below to help you.

31

GET TO KNOW READING GEMS

Reading Gems is a series of books that has been written for children who are learning to read. The books have been created in consultation with a literacy specialist.

The books fit into four levels, with each level getting more challenging as a child's confidence and reading ability grows. The simple text and fun illustrations provide gradual, structured practice of reading. Most importantly, these books are good stories that are fun to read!

Level 1 is for children who are taking their first steps into reading. Story themes and subjects are familiar to young children, and there is lots of repetition to build reading confidence.

Level 2 is for children who have taken their first reading steps and are becoming readers. Story themes are still familiar but sentences are a bit longer, as children begin to tackle more challenging vocabulary.

Level 3 is for children who are developing as readers. Stories and subjects are varied, and more descriptive words are introduced.

Level 4 is for readers who are rapidly growing in reading confidence and independence. There is less repetition on the page, broader themes are explored and plot lines straddle multiple pages.

The Weather Monster follows Joe as he sets off to meet the weather monster. It explores themes of making friends and different types of weather.

Level 4

Joe and Ron set off back down the mountain. It doesn't take long with Ron carrying Joe all the way.

When the villagers see the weather monster, they are scared.

"Meet my friend, Ron," shouts Joe.
Ron grins his toothy grin and the sun comes out.

"Hello, everyone," he says.

Longer sentences ✓

Wide range of vocabulary ✓

Varied and descriptive language ✓

Pictures provide opportunity for further discussion ✓